This is Doctor Daisy. She is a very
good doctor, and she works hard
to keep all her patients healthy
here in Story Town.

A catalogue record for this book is available from the British Library

Published by Ladybird Books Ltd
80 Strand London WC2R 0RL
A Penguin Company

13 15 17 19 20 18 16 14 12

Illustrations © Emma Dodd MMII

LADYBIRD and the device of a Ladybird are trademarks of Ladybird Books Ltd

Little Workmates

Doctor Daisy

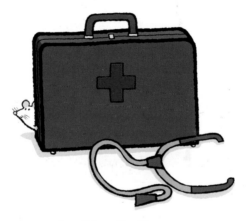

by Mandy Ross
illustrated by Emma Dodd

Ladybird

Doctor Daisy got up early one morning.

"It's Healthy Heart Day today," she said, and off she went for a healthy run before breakfast.

Doctor Daisy ate a very healthy breakfast.

"Mustn't forget my stethoscope," she said as she set off for work.

"I'll be listening to lots of hearts today."

Story Town Surgery was busy. Lots of people had come for a Healthy Heart check-up.

The first patient was Fireman Fergus. His heart sounded very healthy...

Ba-doum Ba-doum

"Do you get lots of exercise?" asked Doctor Daisy, "Exercise is good for hearts."

The next patient was
PC Polly. Her heart
sounded very healthy, too...

Ba-doum
Ba-doum

"Do you get lots
of exercise?"
asked Doctor Daisy.

The last patient that day
was Builder Bill. But his heart
sounded very strange...

Eek! Eek! Eek!

"That sounds like a very
healthy... MOUSE!"
shouted Doctor Daisy.

Suddenly Builder Bill's pet mouse jumped out of his dungaree pocket and down onto the floor.

"Eek!" shrieked Doctor Daisy.

Builder Bill chased the mouse all round the surgery. At last he caught it.

"I can see you get LOTS of exercise," said Doctor Daisy.

"Plenty," said Builder Bill, "...chasing this mouse!"

Then Doctor Daisy had
another go at listening to
Builder Bill's heart.

Ba-doum
Ba-doum

"That sounds like a
very healthy HEART!"
said Doctor Daisy.

When she got home for her tea, Doctor Daisy found a heart-shaped card on her doorstep. Inside it said,

Thanks for looking after our hearts, Doctor Daisy.

Bill x

Fergus xx

Polly xx

 This is Fireman Fergus. He is a brave firefighter and he has a good head for heights.

This is Nurse Nancy. She works hard looking after the patients at Story Town Hospital.

 This is Builder Bill. He is a very good builder and his houses never fall down.

This is Queen Clara. She is a very good queen and all the people of Story Town love her.

 This is Postman Pete. He loves delivering letters and parcels to everyone in Story Town.